The
Rain Cloud

Story and Pictures by

Mary Rayner

Atheneum New York
1980

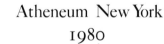

For Eric

Also by Mary Rayner
Mr and Mrs Pig's Evening Out
Garth Pig and the Icecream Lady

Once upon a time there was a rain cloud. One warm and sunny day in May it floated over the sea. . .

getting fuller and fuller until it came
to the land.

It felt very full and wanted very much
to rain.

On the beach there were children
making sand-castles or paddling in
the sea.

Their mothers looked up from their deck-chairs and saw the cloud. They put away their knitting and gathered up the clothes: the sweaters, the shoes and the socks.

"Come along, children," they shouted, "it's going to rain."

But the children cried, "Oh no, we haven't finished our castles."

So the rain cloud thought: I won't rain yet. It sailed on over the land until it saw rows of houses and gardens. In the gardens were lines of washing hung out to dry.

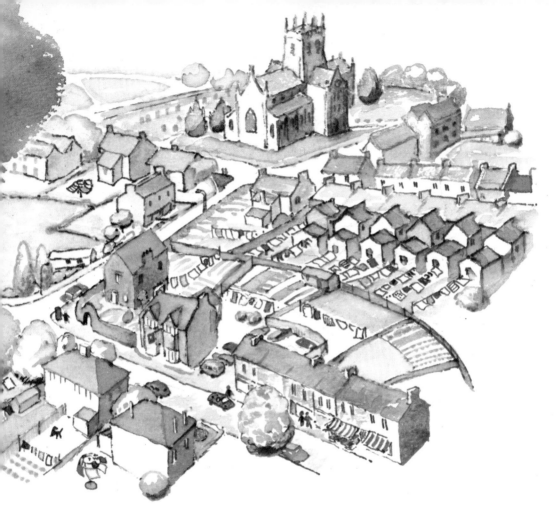

Ah, thought the cloud, that's washing, isn't it.
I'll wash it for them. That should please them.

And it began to rain lightly down all over the clothes.

But as soon as the rain started to fall, everyone ran out of their houses to bring in the washing. They looked up at the sky and frowned. "It's raining and the washing isn't dry yet."

Oops, thought the cloud, my mistake, and it stopped raining and went a little further.

It saw a baby lying fast asleep in a garden.

Just then the baby's two brothers came out of
the house with their mother. She looked up at
the cloud. "Oh," she said, "I've only just got
him to sleep and now it's going to rain. If I pull
up the hood I shall wake him up."

So the rain cloud thought: I mustn't rain yet.
It floated on over the fields and rivers until it
came to a steep hill. There were some people
climbing up it.

When they reached the top they sat down to
have a picnic. They looked up and saw the
cloud.

"Oh no," they said. "Any minute now it's
going to rain and that will spoil everything."

Oh dear, thought the cloud, and it tried very hard not to. By now it was absolutely bursting, so it hurried on until it came to a village where it saw a man up a ladder, painting a house.

The man looked up and clenched his fist and swore out loud.

Hey, thought the cloud, upset, that's not fair, and before it could stop itself, a burst of drops was spattering down. The cloud couldn't help thinking what a grand noise they made drumming on the tiles, and tried to aim them all onto the roof.

But the painter began to climb down the ladder, leaving all the new wet paint half finished. "New paint'll all spoil," he growled. "It can't start raining, forecast was dry."

Oh can't it, thought the cloud, but then it
looked again at the paint and thought it would
be a pity to spoil it, so it scurried on, over the
wide countryside.

Where *can* I rain then? it wondered.

It could see the cows in the fields, tiny black
and white specks on the green ground, and then
way below, in a brown field, a tractor, moving
as slowly as an ant. It could hear the sound of
the engine, very faint and far away.

It came down much lower to have a better
look, and the farmer on the tractor looked
up and saw it.

He smiled.

"Ah good, reckon it's going to rain. Just what my wheat needs right now to make it grow tall and strong," he said.

The rain cloud was so pleased that at last someone wanted it to rain that it let go, and the rain came swooshing down on the dry earth.

It made the brown field beautifully dark and muddy, it made the green ones wet and squelchy. . .

and for a short
and glorious while,
it made streams in
all the lanes and
lakes in all the roads.

The cloud felt much better. . .

and the farmer that year had the best crop of
wheat that he had ever had.